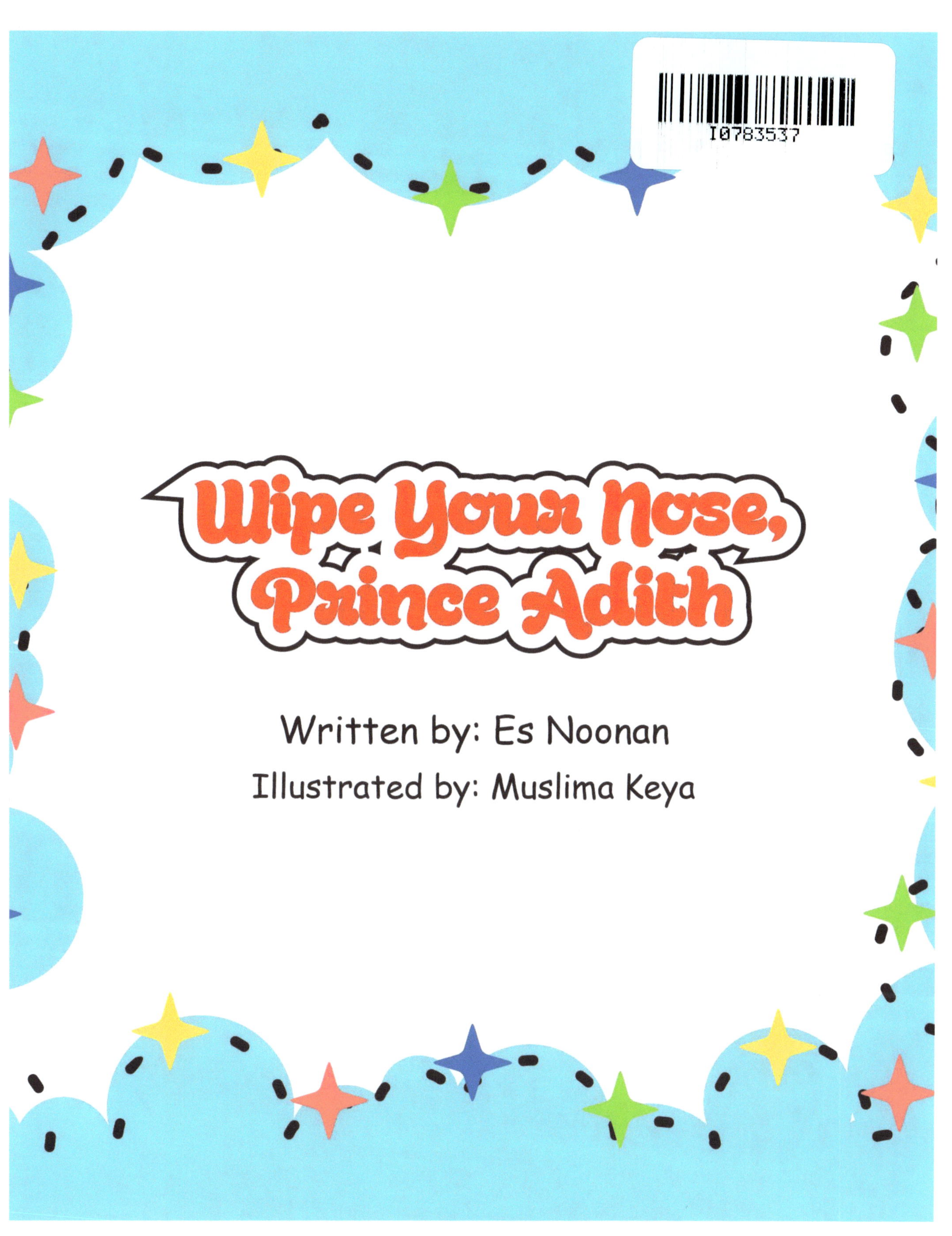

Wipe Your Nose, Prince Adith

Written by: Es Noonan

Illustrated by: Muslima Keya

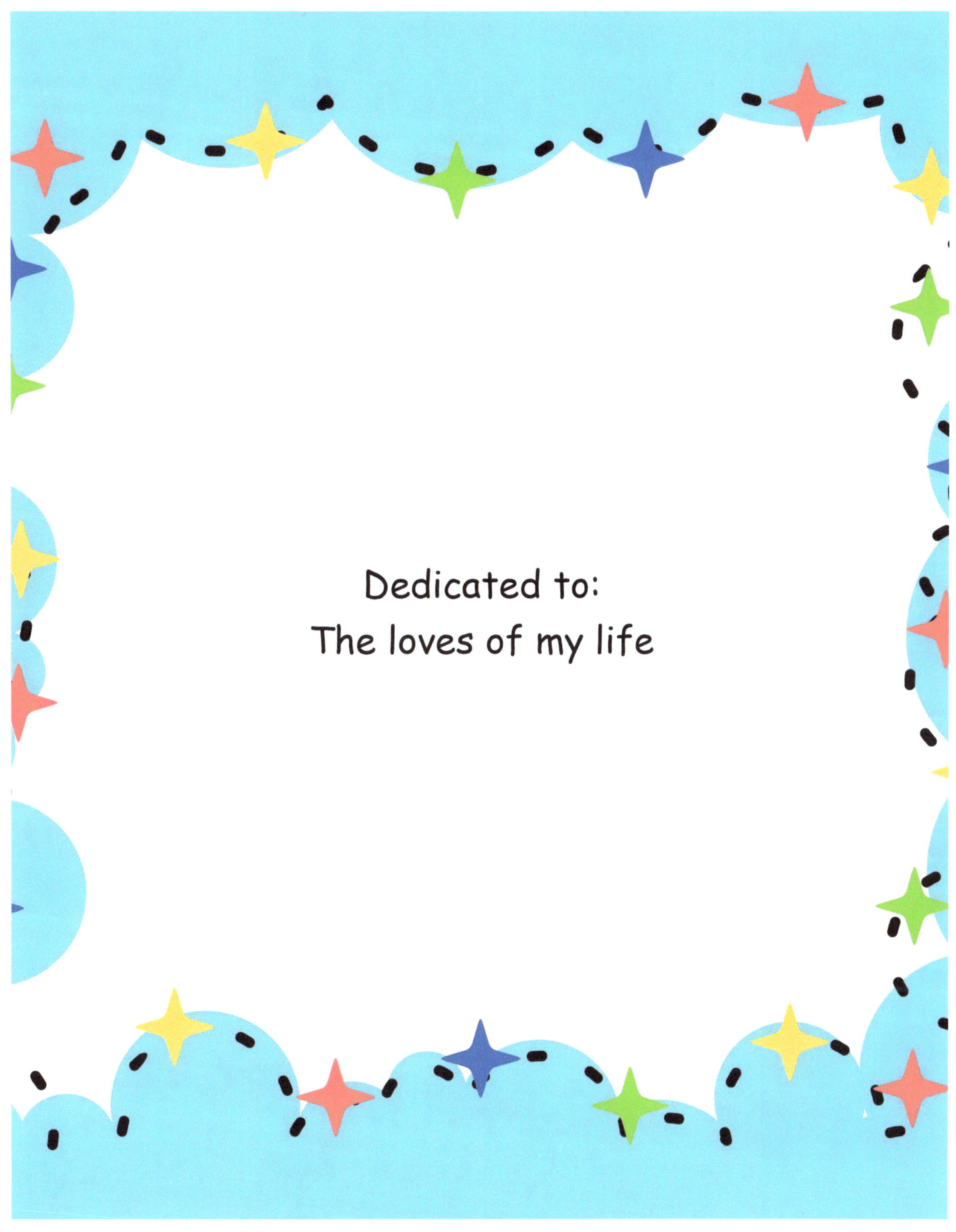

Dedicated to:
The loves of my life

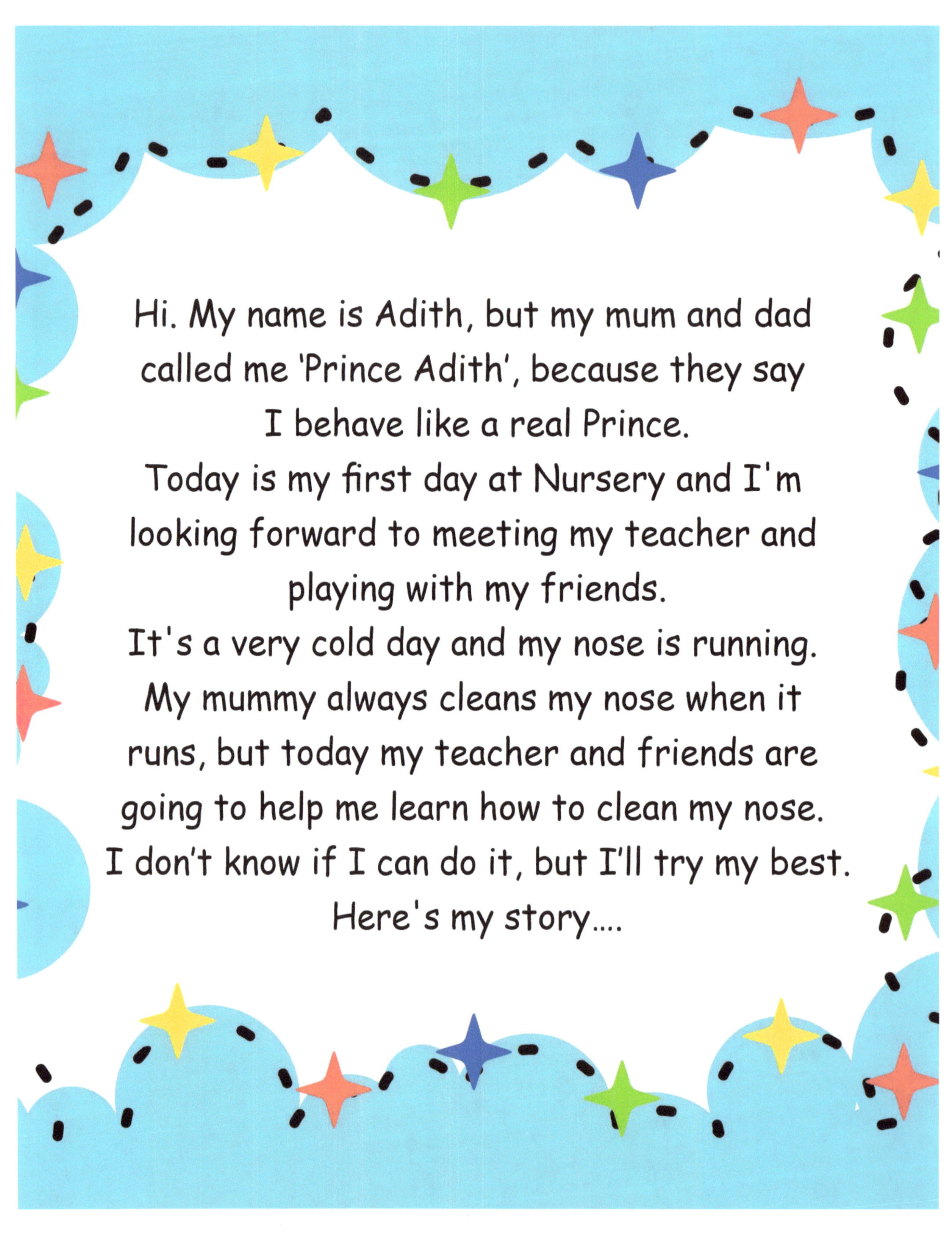

Hi. My name is Adith, but my mum and dad called me 'Prince Adith', because they say I behave like a real Prince.
Today is my first day at Nursery and I'm looking forward to meeting my teacher and playing with my friends.
It's a very cold day and my nose is running. My mummy always cleans my nose when it runs, but today my teacher and friends are going to help me learn how to clean my nose. I don't know if I can do it, but I'll try my best.
Here's my story....

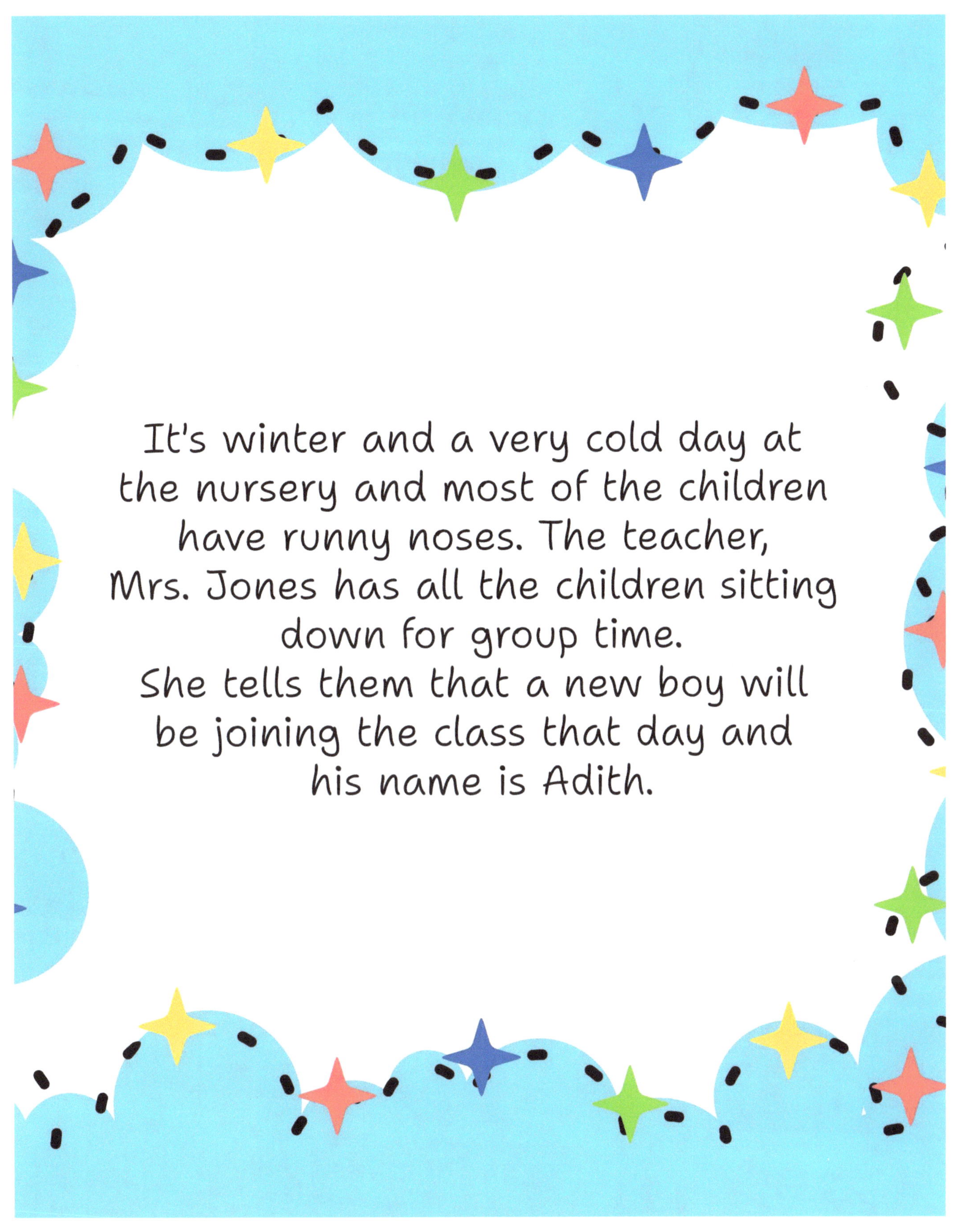

It's winter and a very cold day at
the nursery and most of the children
have runny noses. The teacher,
Mrs. Jones has all the children sitting
down for group time.
She tells them that a new boy will
be joining the class that day and
his name is Adith.

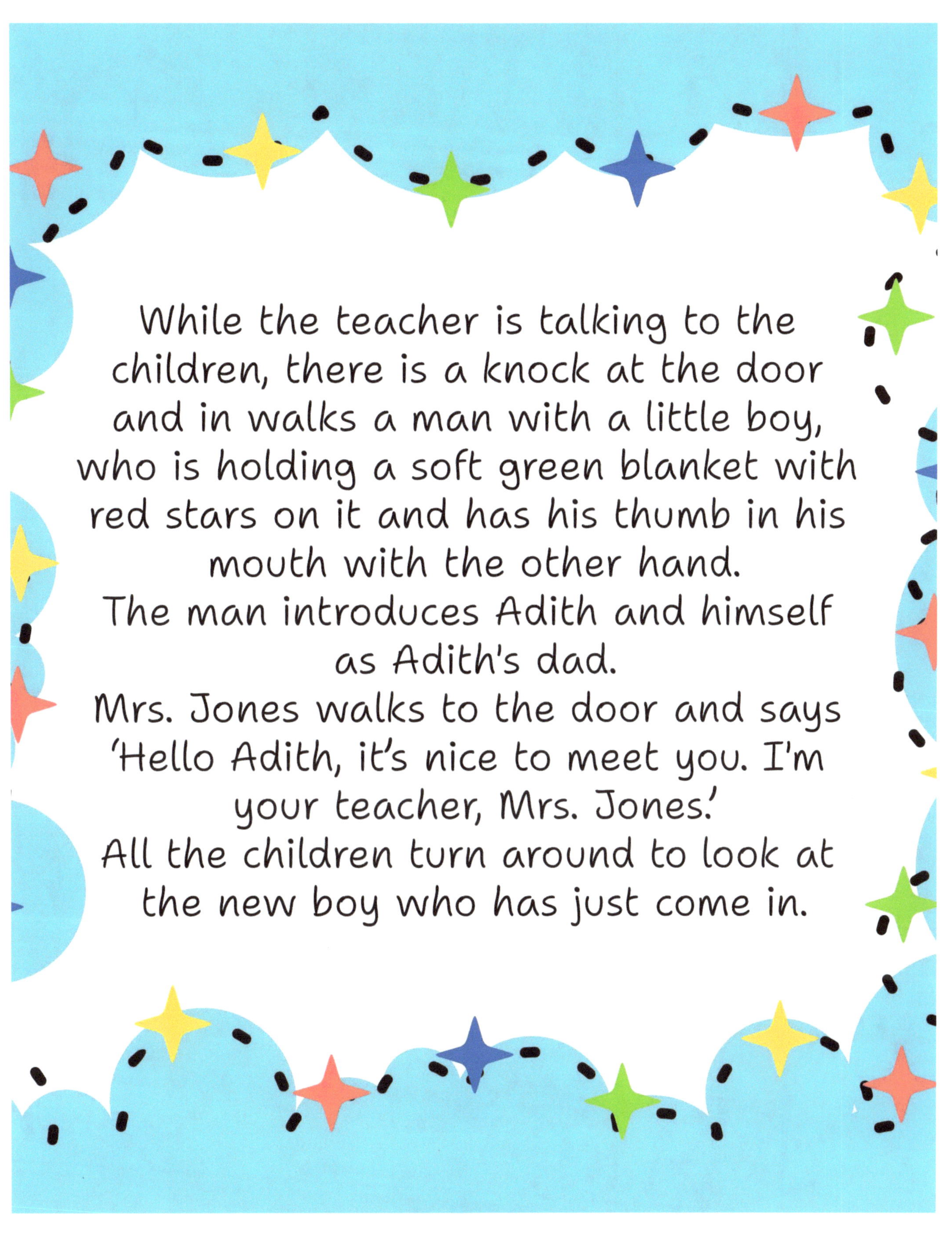

While the teacher is talking to the children, there is a knock at the door and in walks a man with a little boy, who is holding a soft green blanket with red stars on it and has his thumb in his mouth with the other hand.
The man introduces Adith and himself as Adith's dad.
Mrs. Jones walks to the door and says 'Hello Adith, it's nice to meet you. I'm your teacher, Mrs. Jones.'
All the children turn around to look at the new boy who has just come in.

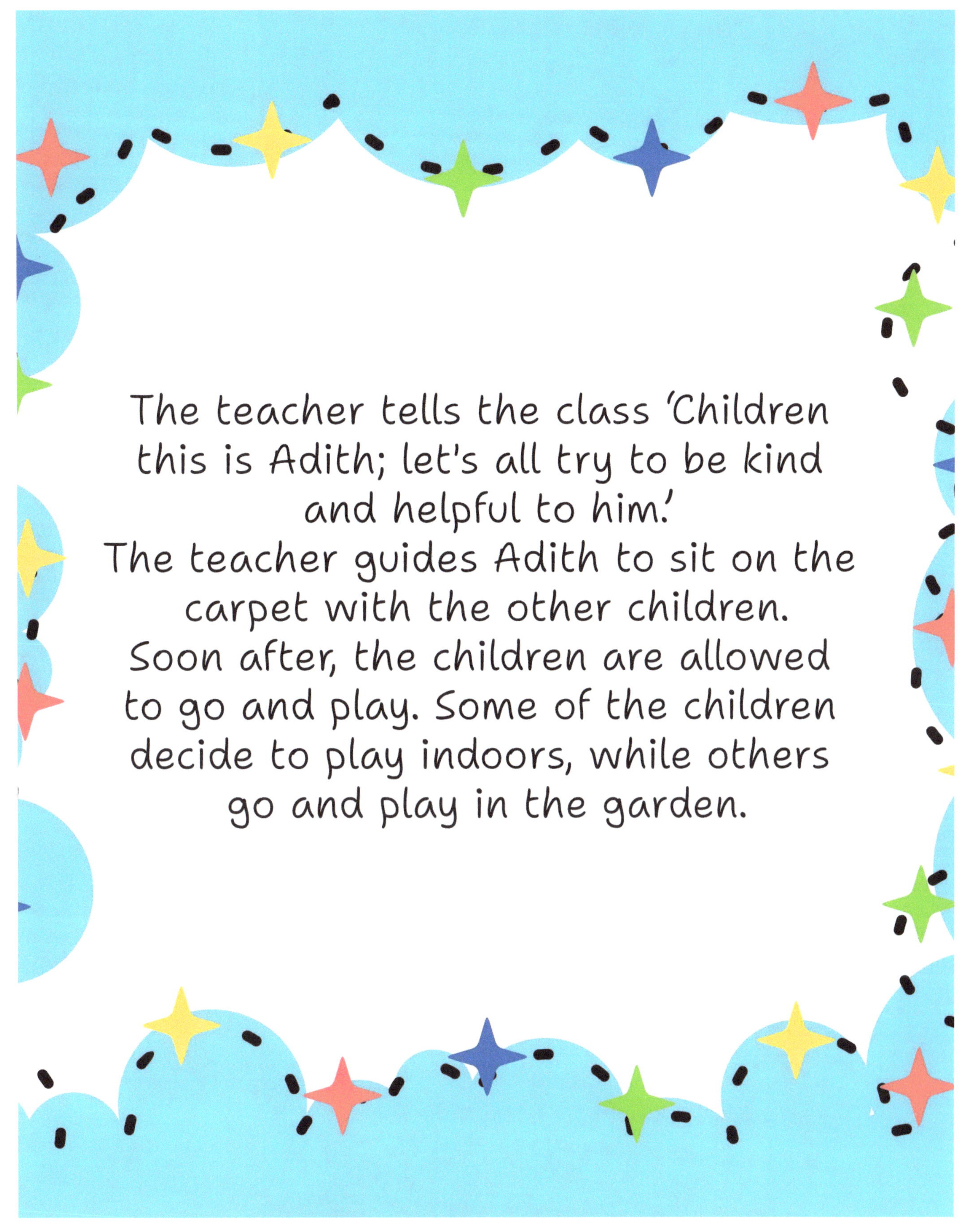

The teacher tells the class 'Children this is Adith; let's all try to be kind and helpful to him.'
The teacher guides Adith to sit on the carpet with the other children.
Soon after, the children are allowed to go and play. Some of the children decide to play indoors, while others go and play in the garden.

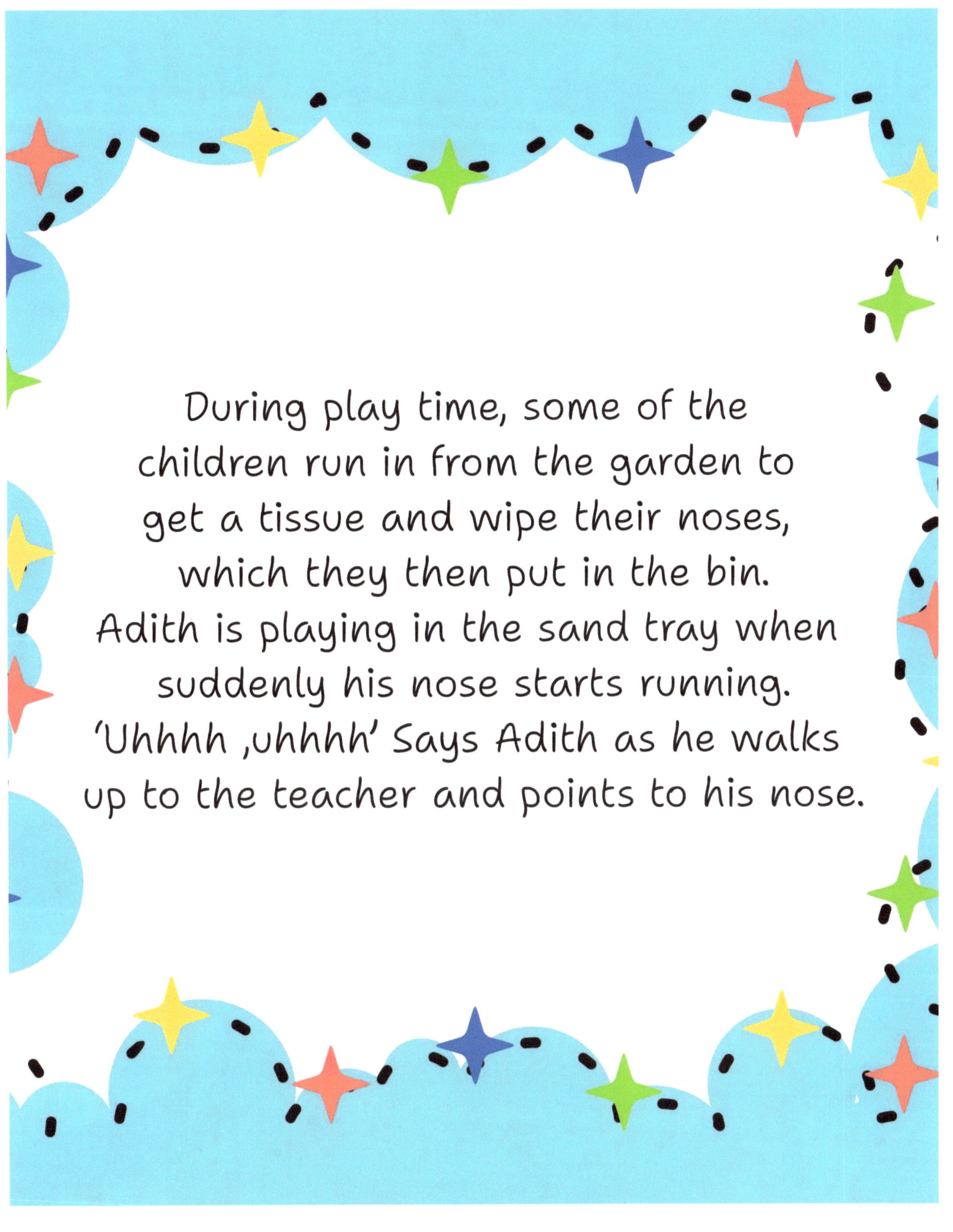

During play time, some of the
children run in from the garden to
get a tissue and wipe their noses,
which they then put in the bin.
Adith is playing in the sand tray when
suddenly his nose starts running.
'Uhhhh ,uhhhh' Says Adith as he walks
up to the teacher and points to his nose.

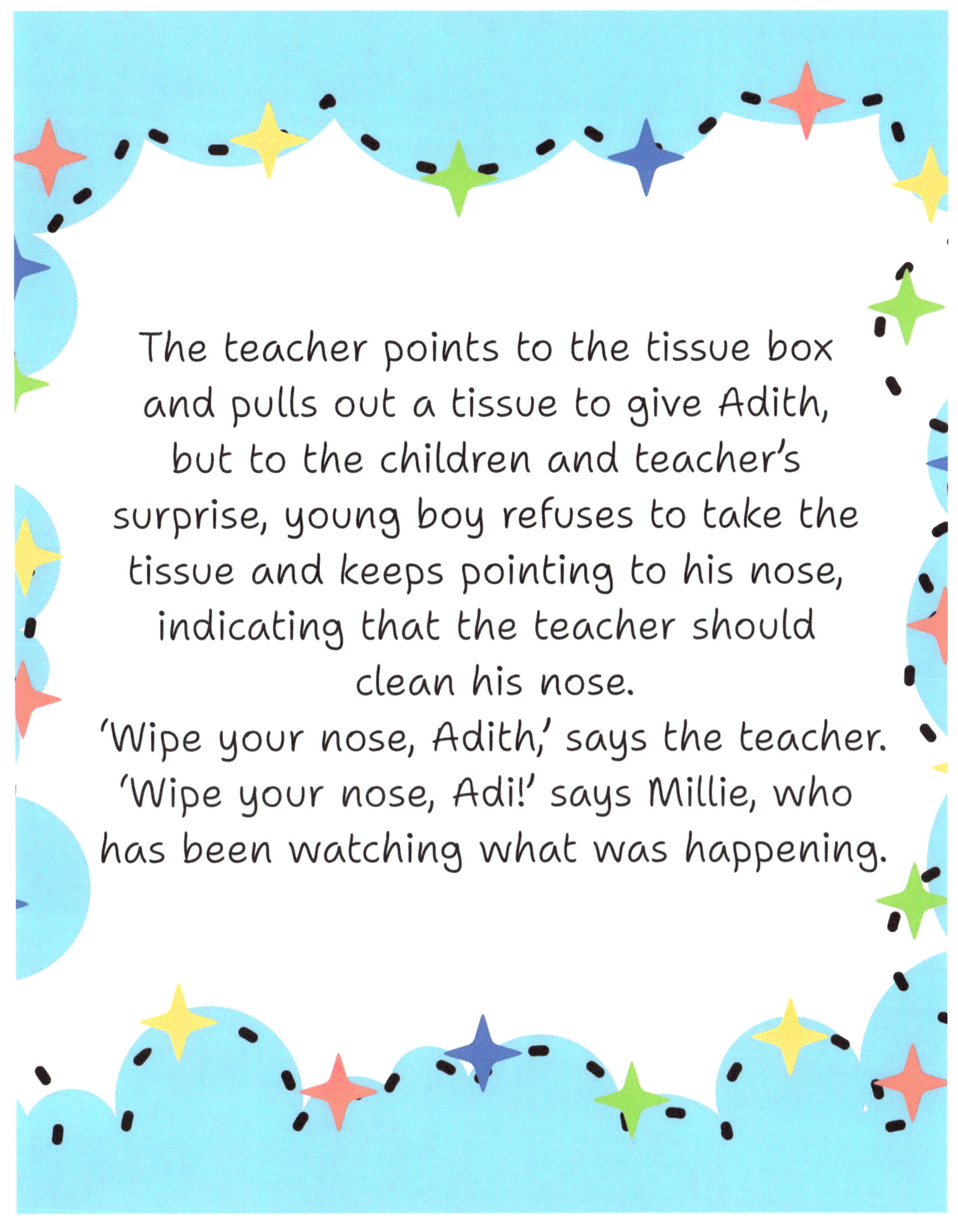

The teacher points to the tissue box and pulls out a tissue to give Adith, but to the children and teacher's surprise, young boy refuses to take the tissue and keeps pointing to his nose, indicating that the teacher should clean his nose.

'Wipe your nose, Adith,' says the teacher. 'Wipe your nose, Adi!' says Millie, who has been watching what was happening.

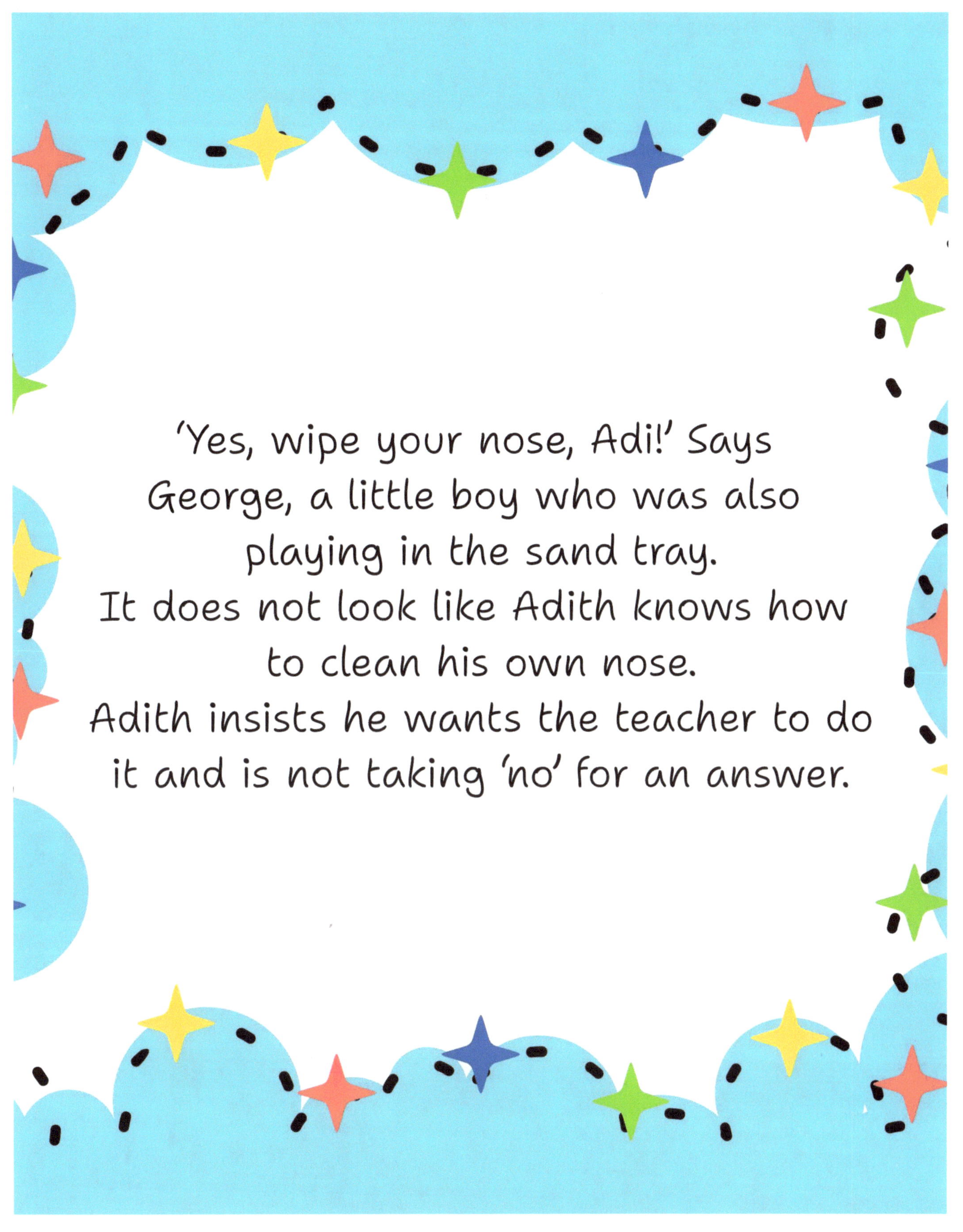

'Yes, wipe your nose, Adi!' Says
George, a little boy who was also
playing in the sand tray.
It does not look like Adith knows how
to clean his own nose.
Adith insists he wants the teacher to do
it and is not taking 'no' for an answer.

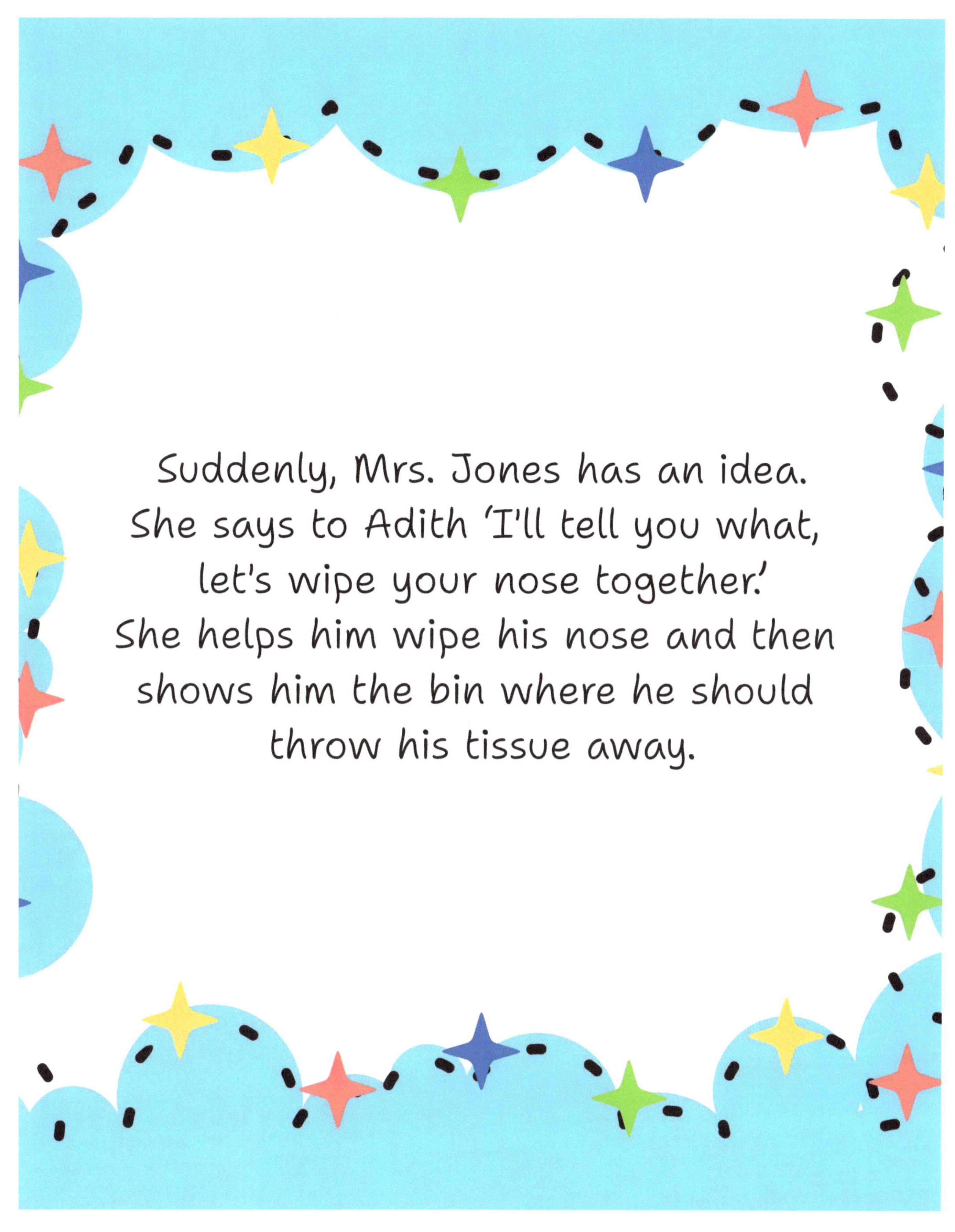

Suddenly, Mrs. Jones has an idea.
She says to Adith 'I'll tell you what,
let's wipe your nose together.'
She helps him wipe his nose and then
shows him the bin where he should
throw his tissue away.

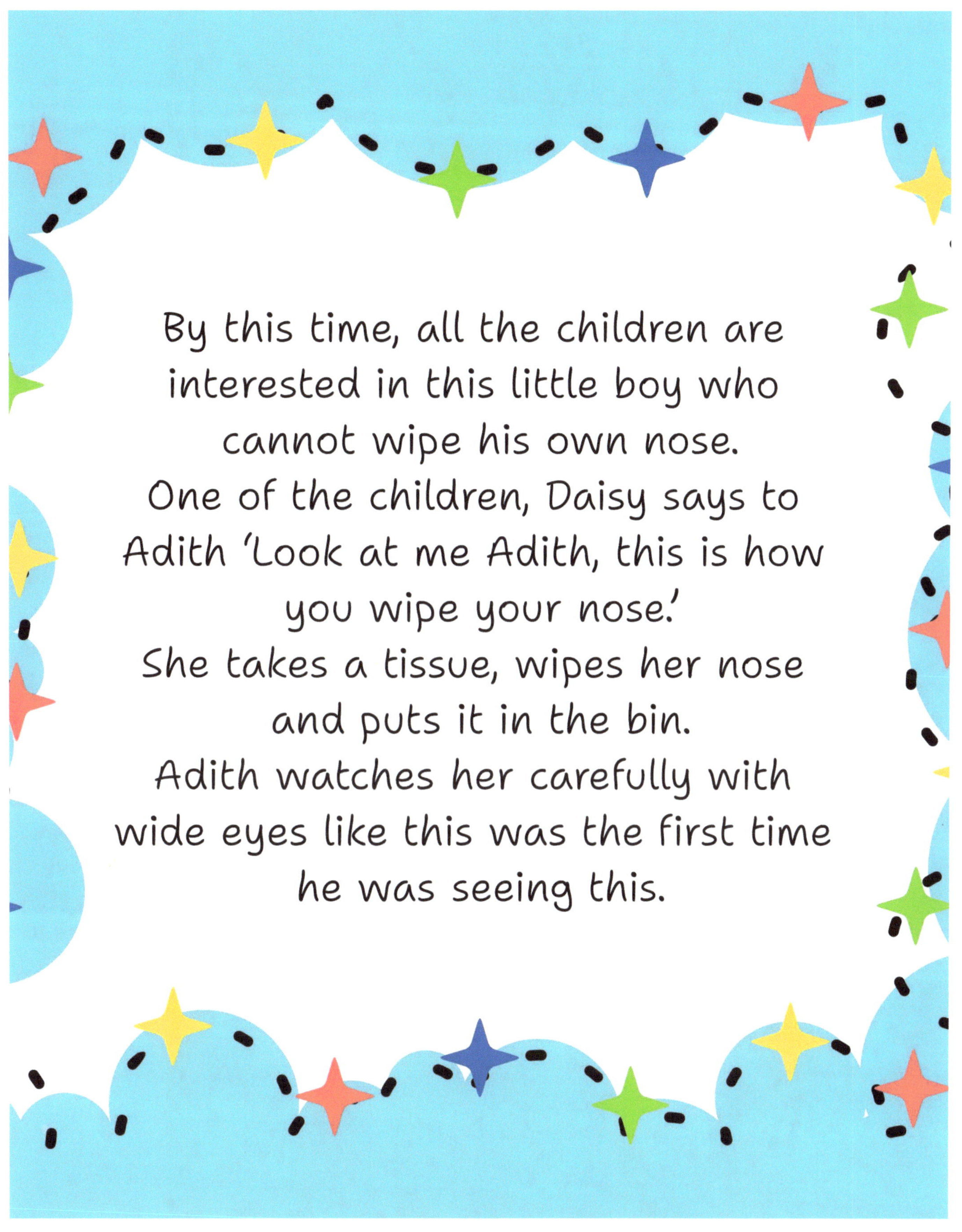

By this time, all the children are
interested in this little boy who
cannot wipe his own nose.
One of the children, Daisy says to
Adith 'Look at me Adith, this is how
you wipe your nose.'
She takes a tissue, wipes her nose
and puts it in the bin.
Adith watches her carefully with
wide eyes like this was the first time
he was seeing this.

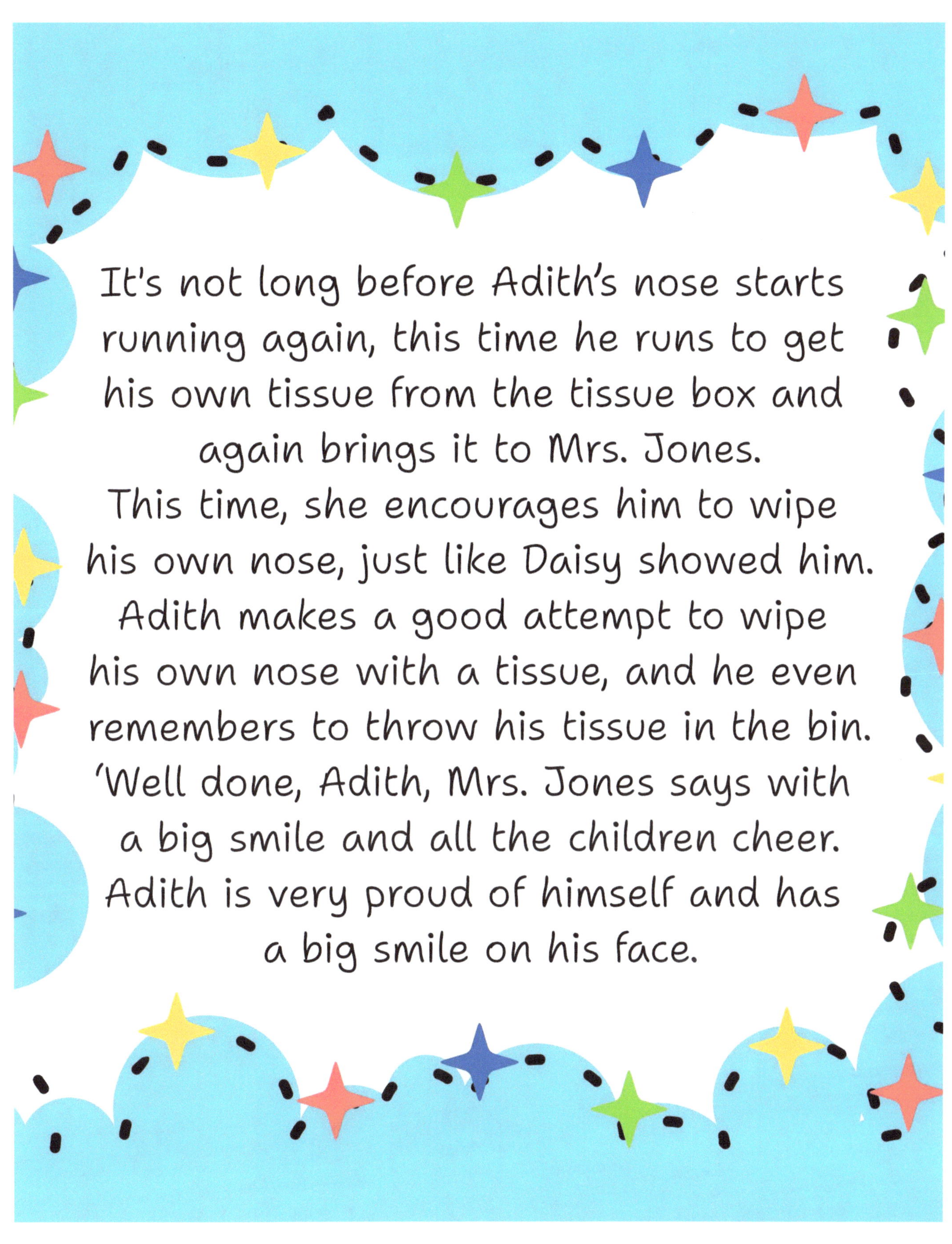

It's not long before Adith's nose starts
running again, this time he runs to get
his own tissue from the tissue box and
again brings it to Mrs. Jones.
This time, she encourages him to wipe
his own nose, just like Daisy showed him.
Adith makes a good attempt to wipe
his own nose with a tissue, and he even
remembers to throw his tissue in the bin.
'Well done, Adith, Mrs. Jones says with
a big smile and all the children cheer.
Adith is very proud of himself and has
a big smile on his face.

Soon after this event, the children sit down for a story, as it's nearly home time. Shortly after, there's a knock on the door. Adith's dad has returned to take Adith home.

However, just before he leaves Adith takes a tissue from the tissue box, cleans his nose and throws it in the bin. Adith's dad looks surprised, and he smiles as he leads Adith out the door. Adith waves to the other children and his teacher, Mrs. Jones as he walks out of the nursery feeling very proud of himself.

The End